T0368438

AuthorHouse™
1663 Liberty Drive
Bloomington, IN 47403
www.authorhouse.com
Phone: 1 (800) 839-8640

Published by AuthorHouse 10/29/2015

ISBN: 978-1-5049-5521-8 (sc)
978-1-5049-5522-5 (e)

Library of Congress Control Number: 2015916954

Print information available on the last page.

Any people depicted in stock imagery provided by Thinkstock are models,
and such images are being used for illustrative purposes only.
Certain stock imagery © Thinkstock.

This book is printed on acid-free paper.

Because of the dynamic nature of the Internet, any web addresses or links contained in this book may have changed
since publication and may no longer be valid. The views expressed in this work are solely those of the author and do
not necessarily reflect the views of the publisher, and the publisher hereby disclaims any responsibility for them.

authorHOUSE®

MR. B
AND HIS
HORSES

Doreen B.

Contents

Dedication:

I would like to dedicate this book to my amazing husband Nelson and to our son Alan. Also, in my memory of our dear son Christopher – who left this world far too soon - 7/21/1968 – 7/30/2011. We miss your companionship, your hugs and your beautiful smile. We will remember you and love you always.

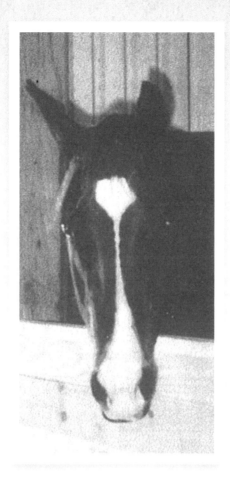

Skippy

Hi, y'all.

My name is Skippy, although my registered name is Skip-A-Mydarling. I was born at the Vance Ranch in Huntsville, Texas, in 1994. I spent my first four years there. My days at the ranch were wonderful. I got the best of care, and my mother, two siblings, and several friends were there with me. I sure was a happy camper.

Unfortunately, Mr. Vance (my owner) was growing older and had to reduce his workload, so I was put up for adoption in 1999. At first, I was very sad to think I would be separated from my mother and sisters. Then, after I thought about it for a while, the move seemed to be a bit exciting. I would get to travel and make new friends, so I guessed it wouldn't be so bad after all. Anyway, I had no choice, so I decided to just deal with it when the time came.

In July of 1999, the neighboring town of Huntsville, Texas, was having a special event called The Yellow Rose of Texas. It was a small-town affair for horse adoptions and the sale of all kinds of western goods—saddles, horse blankets, reins, halters, and the like. There were hundreds of people there and several beautiful animals.

It took quite a while for all the horses to get registered for the sale. I could see the sadness in Mr. Vance's eyes as he was given my registration number and was told to lead me to the holding pen to join all the other horses. He stayed there with me, brushing and petting me until the announcer called my number.

Then off we went into the show ring, where the prospective owners were waiting to look me over. That's when I started to get more than a little frightened. Luckily, I didn't have long to wait; I was chosen almost immediately by a very pleasant-looking man. He seemed happy and laughed a lot. To me that was a good sign.

I was led off to a private stall to wait for the final arrangements to be made. Then my journey to my new home began. My new owner was known as Mr. B by many of his friends and acquaintances. He and his wife had acquired forty-plus acres in the small city of Katy, Texas, about thirty miles west of Houston. After completing all the paperwork, Mr. B loaded me into the trailer, and we headed for my new home.

The trip from Huntsville to Katy was tiring, and I looked forward to getting out of the trailer to stretch my legs and run around a bit. When we arrived at the Diamond B, I was very surprised to see that although there were lots of pastures, there was no house or barn; a huge corral was set up for me. In a large section of land close to the corral was a cement pad. Workers had started building a framework around it for a new barn.

I noticed right away there were no other animals except for a large, mixed-breed dog named Shelby. She was no beauty but was friendly; I think she was as pleased to see me as I was to see her. We soon became best friends.

At first, I was lonely in my new home. Mr. B didn't live on the property, but he was there most day to make sure the barn workers were following his instructions and to make sure I had everything I needed.

Mr. B and Skippy

Mr. B, Skippy, and Shelby

Skippy in Stall

New Barn

The barn was completed within two weeks, and I had a huge forty-by-sixty-foot barn all to myself. It was wonderful! Mr. B worked very hard and quickly prepared a beautiful stall for me. It was twelve by twelve feet and had a nice sandy floor. I felt like a queen with my own new castle. I knew then that I would have a long, comfortable life.

Mr. B must have known I was a little lonely, even though Shelby tried to keep me entertained. She liked to stand on her back legs and rub noses with me. Mr. B got a kick out of that; he even took some pictures of us. My favorite shows me wearing a straw cowboy hat. I think Shelby was jealous because she didn't have a hat too. She said I looked silly, but I thought I looked pretty darn good.

Anyway, Mr. B contacted Mr. Vance and made arrangements to adopt another one of his horses. This one was called Freckles; she was a really sweet horse, and we had been best friends when I lived at the Vance Ranch. Mr. Vance arranged with my mister to bring Freckles to the Diamond B Ranch. Unfortunately, Freckles got injured pretty severely, and Mr. Vance could not deliver her as he had promised. I felt really bad. I just hoped Freckles would be okay.

It wasn't long before my mister went to a county fair where more horses were up for adoption. Needless to say, I was real excited and very curious. I was sure Mr. B would bring home a very likeable companion for me.

The day passed slowly. Finally, I saw the horse trailer coming down the driveway, and I could see there was a horse inside. I thought, *Gosh, I hope the new horse will like me! We can have so much fun together, racing and playing in the pasture like I used to with my siblings.*

Mr. B parked the trailer right outside the barn about twenty feet from me. I whinnied to the other horse so she would feel welcome. Then Mr. B opened the back gate to the trailer and opened the door.

Out jumped a tiny filly. Oh, how cute she was! She jumped and pranced all around like a jackrabbit. She certainly was happy to get out of that trailer. (I knew the feeling.)

Then Mr. B unloaded the filly's mother. What a great-looking mare! She had very pretty head, with a long, flowing mane and a short forelock. I could see she was anxious about her little offspring, but I knew Mr. B would be very gentle with her and her filly.

The new mare's name was Star, and right off the mister named the filly Prancer. And that certainly was a good name for her.

It was so nice to have company, even though Star was not up to playing and racing; she was too busy with her little one. Star was still lots of company for me, and watching Prancer made me want to have a foal of my own.

The following year I did have my first foal, and we call her Peppy. She is gorgeous: four white socks and a white diamond with a blaze on her face. She is a real joy, a very happy filly, and we are all very proud of her.

Skippy in Cowboy Hat

Peppy

Peppy

Mr. B finished building four more stalls. One, a double stall, twelve by twenty-four feet, was for the mares when they had their foals. I was the first to use it—when I had Peppy. It was great! There was so much room, my little filly was able to run around and play with very little supervision. I didn't have to worry about her getting hurt or roaming away and getting lost. We spent her first three days in that stall, and then we were put out to our own pasture.

Our life was great. We had good food, good shelter and pastures, plus lots of loving care and companionship. Star was a good friend, and Prancer and Peppy got along fine.

It wasn't too long before Mr. B decided to go to another horse adoption. This time, he came back with a larger trailer, and it looked like there were two horses inside. Once again, I whinnied to let the new horses know they were welcome.

Mr. B parked the trailer a bit closer this time, so Star, Prancer, Peppy, and I could all have a better view from the barn. He opened the back gate of the trailer and led out a white-and-brown paint horse. She was a good-looking mare—muscular, with a pretty face. Right behind her jumped out a tiny foal who looked to be just a few days old. He was a cutie with white stockings, a white blaze, and a golden mane and tail.

My mister led them to the larger stall so they could stretch their legs and rest. I was sure that little one was exhausted.

Then Mr. B returned to the trailer and unloaded the other horse. Wow! What a beauty this one was! She had a bright-red coat with white stockings and a white blaze. I was impressed and a bit jealous, and so was Star.

It took a little while for the mister to get the new horses settled. He set them up in their new, clean stalls, with water and some sweet grain. Mr. B also made sure they had enough fresh hay to last them through the night. It didn't take long for all our new friends to settle down and rest.

The next morning, our mister was there bright and early. I soon learned that the paint horse was called Dee, and Mr. B named her young colt Don Dee. The big red mare was called Secret. They were all friendly and wanted to learn about the ranch, their new owner, and his wife. It wasn't long before we all became good friends, just like a family.

A few months passed, and I had another little filly, Glory. I hate to brag, but she was the prettiest one of the bunch. I didn't tell Peppy that; she was a little jealous of her new sister. I did my best to treat them equally, but as we all know, the younger ones always need more attention.

Glory (three days old)

Glory (three days old)

Peppy and I had made a habit of finding a nice grassy section in the pasture and lying down, side by side, for our afternoon nap. Glory always manages to squeeze in between us. Peppy didn't like this idea at all, but she was very patient with her sibling and let her get away with it.

My life at the ranch with Mr. B has been very rewarding, I am so thankful that Mr. B chose me. He has given my family and me a very pleasant and comfortable life. I hope it will last forever.

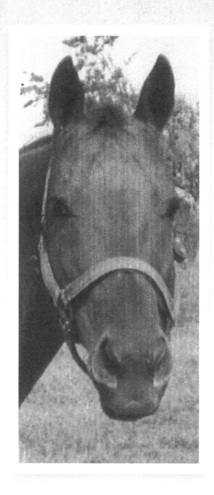

Star

Hello there.

My name is Star. Actually, my registered name is Starette Goldseeker, and I was born in Woodward, Kansas, on March 18, 1994. I lived at my birthplace for the first two years of my life, then my owners made a trade with one of their relatives in Wichita, Kansas. After three weeks of training there, I was moved again, this time to Sanger, Texas. My stay there lasted only four weeks.

I was beginning to get an inferiority complex. I thought nobody wanted me, and I felt like I may never have a real home. Then, on August 6, 1996, I was placed with a family in Longview, Texas. By then, I was very travel weary. They were super-nice people, and I do believe they liked me.

After two and a half years, I gave birth to a filly. She was so precious, but what a handful! She jumped around all over the place, so full of life—and was a real joy to be around.

My time in Longview was a very pleasant three years. I thought I had found my permanent home with them, but that was not to be. My owners were going through a real hard time financially and decided to give me up for adoption, especially when they became aware that I was going to have another foal. My young filly was just five months old.

In October of 1999, when the foal and horse show came to town, they registered me along with my little one. They said that the filly had to go with me wherever I went. I was very pleased about that. My owners were very kind, pleasant people and had always been very good to me. I knew they had a hard giving us up, but they did what they had to do. I also knew I would miss them terribly.

Once the registration was completed, they gave us a number, and I was taken to the holding pen with my offspring. She wasn't quite as lively, just as if she knew some big changes were coming up. She stayed very close to me. A lot of people kept coming by and checking out the two of us, which was real nerve-racking.

At long last, they called our number, and my owner gently moved us to the front of the line. Two people were trying to win us. Finally they got it down to one person; the other had given up. So, there it was, settled.

Suddenly, the new owner wanted to give my young filly away. My heart was pounding. How could this be happening? My owner had specified that my little one was to stay with me!

The other man stepped in and said he would gladly take both of us. He also said it wasn't right to separate the two of us, because the filly was too young. After a rather heated discussion, the first man gave in. Whew! That sure was scary!

Our new owner was called Mr. B. He was very gentle with the two of us; I think he knew how frightened we were. The staff helped Mr. B load us into the trailer, and off we went to Katy, Texas, to the Diamond B Ranch, home of Mr. B and his wife.

My poor little filly slept all the way. Traffic was heavy, so it took about four hours. I was so pleased when we entered a long driveway. I could see a huge barn close to two large corrals, and there was a horse in one of them. The horse whinnied loudly, and big black dog twirled around, wagging her tail. I was pleased to see that I would have some companionship at my new home.

Mr. B parked the trailer close to the barn, with the other horse watching our every move. When she saw us get out of the trailer, she started running back and forth, whinnying loudly. What a nice welcome for us! I thought we would be great friends, but all I wanted to do was rest. I found all the travel and stress of changing owners very tiring.

My new mister led us to a huge stall—twelve by twenty-four feet—and promptly fed me some sweet grain, cool water, and fresh hay. I knew we had come to a very safe and pleasant home.

The next day, Mr. B showed up bright and early to feed us and to make sure we had everything we needed. He came by the stall and asked me if I wanted a treat. I nodded, and he got a big kick out of that. When he asked me a second time, I stood on my back legs to show off a bit. This really made him happy. I was dancing just for him. From that moment on, I made a point to nod when he asked if I wanted a treat. To get a second one, I did my little dance for him. I don't care for apples or carrots, so he gave me alfalfa cubes, which are the best treat ever.

Mr. B let us stay in the large stall for the better part of that first morning. Then he led us out to the second corral next to the other horse. He had decided to name my filly Prancer, which really suited her. She ran and jumped and pranced all around that new corral. She went so fast, she kept running into all the fences. It didn't take long before she ran into the wire fence and hurt her face badly. But I will let her tell you all about that. She soon found out how to put the brakes on so she wouldn't hurt herself again.

We learned that the horse in the other corral was called Skippy, and her companion, the dog, was Shelby. I was a little worried about how Shelby would treat Prancer, but they got along just fine.

Mr. B made a big fuss over Prancer, and she loved every minute of it. I could see my little filly was going to be spoiled, and that pleased me. When the mister registered my Prancer, he gave her the registered name Goseekastar. What a perfect name for her!

Prancer

Star & Prancer

Time passed very quickly, and over the next few months, I really packed on the pounds. I totally lost my girlish figure. I was anxious to have this new foal and have things get back to normal. When it came time for my foal to be born, Mr. and Mrs. B kept a close watch on me. They hung around the barn constantly. I wanted to surprise them, so when they went for their morning coffee, and I was alone, I let it happen.

Whoopee! Out came a beautiful, large, healthy colt. It didn't take long for him to be up and about. When Mr. and Mrs. B returned with their coffee, there he was, wide-eyed and bushy tailed—as cute as a button.

I was extremely proud of my newborn and was glad he was a male because that's what my mister wanted. It didn't take long to find a name for him. He was so big—just like the state he was born in—my mister decided to call him Texas.

Prancer was very curious about all the excitement. She peeked into the stall and saw the new addition, and she didn't seem impressed. Texas was cute, but I bet she thought she was cuter.

Texas

Star

Star and Texas in corral

Prancer was used to being number one, and now she had to share that spot with her sibling. It was going to be quite different with Texas around.

Texas and I spent the next three days resting in our big stall. On the morning of the fourth day, Mr. B brushed both Texas and me. My little colt was a bit leery at first, but once he saw me getting brushed, he let the mister brush him, too. After our session of brushing and petting, the mister led us out to one of the large corrals.

Prancer was not allowed to join us in the corral, but she was right beside us in the open pasture. She tried to jump the wire fence to get to us, but she didn't make it. The wire was all wrapped around her front hooves and ankles. Of course, she panicked, and that made it worse.

Mr. B rushed out to the corral and quickly cut all the wire from her legs. Her right front leg was badly torn from the pastern to the top of the tendon. It was just awful. Mr. and Mrs. B's veterinarian was on vacation, so they had to clean the wound and dress it themselves.

Prancer was in a great deal of pain, and my mister gave her a series of shots: antibiotics, tetanus, and a painkiller. I felt so helpless! My poor filly was suffering so much, and I could do nothing to help her.

I heard Mr. B say her injuries were so severe, he may have to put her to sleep. But, with a lot of tender, loving care, he nursed her back to good health. It took several months for her to heal completely, and during that time, Prancer and Texas became close. He was very protective of his sister. He spoiled her just like everyone else did, and that pleased me greatly. They spent most of their time together out in the pasture, grooming each other, racing, and playing.

It had taken me quite a while to find my permanent home, but it was worth the wait. I have so much to be thankful for: a nice home and family, lots of TLC, the best of food, my own personal stall, and people that love me. I count my blessings every day.

Texas and Star

Prancer

Hi-ho, y'all!

I'm Prancer, and I was given that name when I first arrived at the Diamond B Ranch. I was just five months old but full of life. I seldom walked or trotted anywhere; I always pranced. Sometimes I would even jump straight up in the air, with all four feet off the ground. I was a very happy filly, and it felt good to stretch and bounce around like that.

My registered title is Goseekastar. I really like both of my names; they are different. Mr. B (my owner) used part of my mother's name when he registered me. Her name is Starette Goldseeker. Her ancestors are both quarter horse and thoroughbred—a nice mix—and she is a real beauty.

My birthplace is Longview, Texas, and I was so young when we left there, I don't remember much about it. I do recall my mother being very nervous about relocating. She had been very happy living in Longview for three years, and she was upset. I knew we would miss the home where I was born; the family had been very good to us.

In October of 1999, when the local fair came to town, she and I were registered for adoption. Once we were registered and given a number, they took us to a holding pen where several horses waited for their numbers to be called.

It was most frightening! I had never been among so many animals at one time. I kept as close as possible to my mother. I kept wishing she had a big pocket so I could jump in there and hide. That day I was not prancing! It was more like snuggling, just as close as I could get.

As the day dragged on, I was beginning to think they had forgotten us. Then our number was called, and we were led out to a ring, where several ranchers waited to look us over. It seemed to be a contest between two men, and finally the one man won. Boy, I was glad that was over!

All of a sudden, the rancher that had won was trying to get someone to take me off his hands. He didn't want me; he only wanted my mother. I was more than frightened; I was completely terrified. I would be lost without her, and I thought, *How could anyone be so unkind?*

Well, the second rancher insisted I should be kept with my mare because I was so young. And, finally, after an extremely loud discussion, the second rancher won; he ended up adopting both of us. I thanked my lucky stars because I don't think the other man would have made a very nice keeper.

Our new owner's name was Mr. B. He was very pleasant and well organized. Once he took care of all the paperwork, he got right back to us. We were loaded into his trailer, and without any hesitation, he took off for the Diamond B Ranch.

After about four hours, we arrived at our destination. I was thrilled when I saw the beautiful barn and pastures. There was another horse there in one of the corrals, who whinnied nonstop as we drove down the long driveway. There was also a large black dog barking and jumping all around, sounding like he was happy to see us.

Prancer, Star & Mr. B

Mr. B led us out of the trailer and got us settled in a large, fresh-smelling stall. It didn't take me long to fall asleep on the clean, sandy floor. It was so nice to be resting in my comfortable new home. I knew I would be happy.

The following day, our mister put us out in one of the fenced corrals. I was so full of energy after my great night's rest that I took off running full speed ahead, not realizing there was fencing all around the corral. I ran right into the wire fencing and cut a big slice off my face from just below my eyes to the tip of my nose. The skin with all the hair was just hanging there.

When Mr. B saw that, he ran to the barn and got the peroxide and some ointment. He rushed back, threw me to the ground, and held me there until he finished doctoring my face. Wow, that man is strong!

My mother just stood and watched. I knew it must be okay because she didn't fuss at all. My wound healed perfectly and left no scar, thanks to my mister's quick action.

Prancer   Star

I enjoyed my new home. The other horse, Skippy, was very friendly. After our first year there, Skippy delivered a nice filly. Mr. B called her Peppy. It was like having a little sister. She was real sweet and liked to play and race around the pasture with me. I really enjoyed her company.

It wasn't too long until Mr. B went to another one of those adoption events. We were all pretty anxious to see what he would bring home. When the day was almost over, a double trailer entered the driveway, and there was Mr. B, all smiles and ready to unload the trailer again.

Prancer

This time it was a very pretty paint: snow white with big brown patches, very muscular, and healthy looking. And she had a very young colt. He was the cutest little guy: sorrel with four white socks and a golden mane and tail.

Right away they were led to their stall so they would have lots of room to stretch their legs. But our mister wasn't finished yet. He led out another horse, a real beauty, which was almost red in color with a white blaze, white stockings, and a golden mane and tail. Mr. B called her Secret.

Time passed quickly, and we were all happy and settled in our own assigned stalls. But one morning, things changed—at least for me they did. My mother delivered a healthy colt.

Mr. and Mrs. B were very pleased; this was the first male colt to be born at the ranch, and they named him Texas. Mr. B kept my mother and Texas separate from the rest of us, even when they were out in the corral. I wasn't allowed to be in there with them, although I was allowed to be in the pasture next to them.

I kept a pretty close watch on them, but I wanted a closer look, so I decided to jump the wire fence and join them. Well, let me tell you, that was one great big mistake. I hadn't gotten halfway over when I found myself all tangled up in that wire. It was wrapped around my front legs. The more I moved, the worse it got.

Lucky for me, our mister was working in the barn and heard all the noise. He yelled at me to be still, but it hurt so much, I kept struggling. He was beside me in a matter of seconds, and he kept telling me to calm down.

Finally, Mr. B got all the wire cut off my legs and helped me to the barn. I was sure I was a goner. I was torn right to the bone. Mr. B called the vet, but he wasn't available. So once again, he had to take care of the wound himself. He gave me several shots, but this time the pain was so severe I felt like banging my head against the wall, and so I did.

My owners checked on me every hour for several days. The healing was very slow. After a month, things were looking pretty good. Six weeks after the accident, I finally got to go out to the pasture for the first time. It was so nice to be outside once more. I will never deal with that wire fence again. I learned my lesson—twice!

Since then I've gotten to know my sibling, Texas, and now I'm enjoying his companionship. He is very protective of me. We groom each other every morning, and we play together all day. My mister has trained me to be a very comfortable ride, and most visitors choose to ride me because I'm so laid-back and gentle. I'm very happy with my life here at the Diamond B Ranch, and I'm glad it was my final destination.

Mr. B & Prancer

Texas

Just call me Texas.

Yup, that's my name! My registered name is Texas Coosa Star, and although they call me Texas, I really am a star.

I was born in Katy, Texas, at the Diamond B Ranch on March 20, 2000, at about 5:30 a.m. I would have arrived earlier, but my owners, Mr. and Mrs. B, kept peeking in to see if I was there yet, and my momma was so shy, she didn't want anyone to watch when she brought me into the world.

I was about 110 pounds, very healthy, and anxious to get out on my own and be able to stretch out a bit. Boy, did that feel good! The first time I stood up, it was really hard. My long, spindly things they call legs were so skinny and wobbly, it took all my strength and courage to even try to stand. Finally, with a lot of coaxing and encouragement from my mother, I made it. At last I was able to look into her eyes, and I could see the pride she felt after bringing me into this world. I vowed then that I would make her very proud of me.

Mrs. B and Texas

Texas and Star

Texas and Star

Before I go further, I would like to tell you about my mother. She is a beautiful bay mare, about fifteen hands high. She is a registered quarter horse with an outstanding background that includes a well-known thoroughbred named Impressive. She has a very pretty head and is extremely intelligent.

When Mr. B wants to give her a special snack, he asks her if she would like a treat. Right away she nods her head, and it pays off; she gets her treat. Then he asks her to dance, and she does it. And, sure enough, she gets another little goodie.

Boy! When I saw that, I realized I could get a special little something, too, if I were to nod my head. I tried it, and it worked! I haven't learned to dance yet. That's going to take some practice. It's not easy to stand up on your back legs and shake your body. I don't know how she does it.

Anyway, I'm so busy strutting around, trying to impress the fillies and the other mares, I haven't had the time for dancing. First things first!

27

I've had my eyes on one filly for the past two years. She really is a beauty, with fantastic bloodlines. Her nickname is Secret, but her registered name is Impressive Exception—and believe me, she is well named. She is a descendent of the great Secretariat. Boy, has she got class. She looks exactly like him (only better).

I have to watch her pretty close because there's a young colt in the next pasture that seems to have his eye on her too. His name is Whiskey, and he tries to get her attention all the time. So I have to keep her busy, hoping she won't notice him.

The first thing I do each morning when we get put out to pasture is check her out. We like to stroll down to the pond then groom each other before we start to play. Secret loves to run, and so do I. I challenge her often. We are both pretty darn fast, though I think I could beat her in an actual race. Oh, how I hope she never finds out I said that!

Since I'm the self-appointed leader of all the horses, I have to be out in front all the time. I just love it. I arch my neck and shake my mane. I often hear my owners say how handsome I am. I don't mean to blow my own horn, but I'm inclined to agree. They also say how intelligent I am. They are well aware of *all* my qualities, even though I have *so* many.

I'm very proud to be one of Mr. and Mrs. B's horses. They provide for my family, my equine friends, and me with a lot of tender, loving care.

I feel very honored to have been called Texas because Texas is a wonderful place to be.

Star and Texas

Star and Texas

Mr. B riding Texas

Secret

Hi there.

My name is Secret. I was born on March 24, 1997, in Many, Louisiana. My registered name is Impressive Exception.

When I was born, my owners were disappointed because I was a filly, even though I was very pretty, with white stockings and a white blaze on my face. They had wanted a colt. So in June of 2000, they put me up for adoption at the Lufkin, Texas, County Fair.

I was very frightened, especially when I saw all the other beautiful young fillies and colts up for adoption too. We were each assigned a number and led to a holding pen to wait for the adoptions to start.

It took hours for my turn to come. My owners paraded me around for what seemed to be a very, very long time. I held my head up high and stood up straight. My heart was pounding so hard, I thought it was going to burst right out of my chest. Then I made up my mind to make the best of it, so I put my best foot forward, said a little prayer, and hoped all would go well.

I didn't have long to wait before Mr. B chose me. He had several other fine-looking fillies to chose from, but I was the lucky one. I liked him right off. He was very gentle and extremely complimentary as he admired my satiny coat. Then he checked my hooves and legs. He seemed pleased with his choice. And believe me, so was I!

I hate to brag, but I do come from a long line of celebrities. I'm sure you've heard of the greatest Triple Crown winner, Secretariat. Well, he just happens to be my great-grandfather! Everyone says I look just like him. They nicknamed him Big Red, and though I'm a female, I'm just as big (or almost) and just as red as he was. I never did get to meet my grandfather, but I have seen several pictures of him. Sure nuff, I do look exactly like him.

After Mr. B completed the paperwork for me, he decided to adopt another horse. This one was a paint with a newborn colt by her side. I was pleased to see that I would have some company at my next home.

Mr. B took care of the paperwork for the paint, and the workers helped to load the three of us into a roomy trailer. Then we headed toward Katy, Texas. That's where my new owner has his ranch. After traveling for about three hours, the truck slowed down and pulled into this long driveway with a good-sized barn at the end.

I could see that there were four horses peering out of their stalls, and all of them whinnied to welcome us. What a pleasant welcome we received!

Mr. B unloaded the three of us from the trailer and got us all settled down for the night. We had our own individual stalls with fresh water and sweet grain. The mister also made sure we all had lots of fresh hay.

Secret & Mr. B

I'm very content here with Mr. B. He's always saying how proud he is to have me and how absolutely gorgeous I am. My mister is an excellent rider, and he really enjoys it when we go for our morning ride. Once in a while, he lets me go into a full gallop. What a thrill I get! We seem to fly! It's so refreshing to feel the soft breeze on my face and my mane flowing gently in the wind.

I wish I had the opportunity to race like my grandfather. I know I would love it, and I'd be extremely good at it. Meanwhile, I've had a lot of happiness and pleasure staying here at the ranch. I have many companions. My favorite is Texas, a strong, handsome young gelding. He is so special and also a strong and proud competitor. We often race through the pasture together. I let him win sometimes, and he seems to like that. It makes him feel good, and if Texas feels good, so do I.

Things were going along just great. I was putting on a lot of weight. When my mister noticed that, he put me on a regular exercise program and cut down on my treats. It didn't seem to help much though. Mr. B was determined to work a few pounds off me, so he increased my exercise schedule. I really liked all the extra attention, and I definitely needed the exercise. But, try as we may, the extra pounds just kept piling on.

One morning, shortly after my grain feeding, I started having very painful stomach cramps. I guessed it was probably just gas or a touch of the flu—but wow! It was the worst one I'd ever had. Anyway, it wasn't long before I realized it was more than the flu. Suddenly, I had a big burst of gas, and there was a loud thump—like a fifty-pound sack of potatoes falling to the ground.

Lo and behold, there was a strange-looking, very scrawny, little filly. She was all eyes, ears, and bones, that poor little thing. No wonder I had put on so much weight.

I was standing there still in shock, not knowing what to do, when my mister came back into the barn to check things out. He stared in disbelief. He was as shocked as I was—maybe even more. How could this possibly happen?

Well, when I thought about it some more, I remembered that, a few months before, my friends (Texas, Star, Dee, and Prancer) and I were all playing tag and leap frog with the horses from the neighboring ranch. The horse called Whiskey did tag me pretty hard a couple of times. Boy, how sneaky can you get! Wow! That's really taking advantage.

Anyway, there we were with a frail little foal. My mister hurried to the feed store to pick up some special feed for the little filly.

Now, let me tell you, it didn't take long for that tiny little thing to stand up and try out those long, boney legs. Once she got standing, she wobbled around, looking for something to eat. At the rate she was moving around, I knew it wouldn't take long for her to put on some weight and be perfectly healthy.

Secret & Tequila

I was right. Within two weeks, she looked normal—actually, quite beautiful. We could see that she was going to be a real beauty. And of course she was built just like me. She had real nice features, with the shape of a tiny white feather on her forehead, a beautiful flaxen mane, and four white stockings, along with a silky red coat. The only thing she had that reminded us of Whiskey was her multicolored tail, and that added to her beauty. My mister decided to name her Tequila, since her sire's name is Whiskey.

Tequila is the sweetest, most affectionate young filly; she just loves people. Any time my mister or his family come into the barn or the pasture, Tequila follows them everywhere. They always make a big fuss over her because she is so loveable.

All my friends, even Texas, welcomed little Tequila. They all took turns spoiling her. It had been a few years since a foal was born here at the ranch, so it was quite a novelty. It took about six weeks for things to get back to normal, but once they did, we all felt blessed to have such a happy, healthy lifestyle. Life here at the ranch has been very rewarding for my friends and me.

Secret

Dee and Secret

Secret & Tequila

Secret

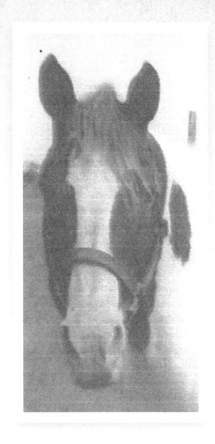

Dee

Hello there.

Let me introduce myself. My name is Dee, and my registered name is Sensational Bee. I am a bit different from the other horses here at the Diamond B Ranch. I'm what they call a paint, and all the others are registered quarter horses. I have a thick, white, and silky coat with a few large, dark-brown patches; my mane and tail are very full and snowy white.

I was born June 29, 1990, in Monroe, Wisconsin, and that September I was adopted by a young couple in Carthage, Mississippi. That's where I received most of my training. I lived there until November 1999, when I was moved to Farmerville, Louisiana. There I was entered in several local equestrian competitions and did well, winning several ribbons. I also delivered a handsome colt at the end of the season.

After I had lived in Louisiana for about a year, my owners decided to sell their farm and all the animals, so when the annual fair came to Lufkin, Texas, in June of 2000, I was put up for adoption along with my two-month-old colt. It was a sad time for all of us. The ranch that had been my home for the past year was far from Lufkin, so we were loaded into the trailer at five in the morning then traveled nonstop for the next four hours.

Upon arrival, we were registered and assigned to our individual stalls to wait for our number to be called. We had an extremely long wait because they took care of the registered quarter horse adoptions first. At one point, it looked like they might have to leave the rest of the horses (paints, thoroughbreds, and others) until the following day. But the officials extended the closing time by two hours. I was thankful because so many animals still needed to be placed.

It was real scary, and my young colt stuck to me like glue. He had no idea what was going on. Many of the ranchers had already made their choices by the time our registration number was called, and a lot of people had gone. I was so pleased when our turn finally came, and there were still a few people interested in us. Finally, a nice-looking, well-dressed cowboy won us. (We knew he was a cowboy because he had one of those cool cowboy hats). He was all smiles, and we were too!

Our new owner quickly completed all the transfer papers then promptly returned to load us into his trailer. I noticed he had another horse in the front section of the trailer. She was a real pretty thing—very proud looking with a reddish coat, white stockings, and a white blaze. She looked almost as scared as we were. It didn't take long for Mr. B to get organized, then off we went to our new home in Katy, Texas.

By then, my young colt was exhausted. I could tell he desperately wanted to lie down and sleep but was afraid to leave my side. He made most of the trip standing.

We were on the road for three and a half hours, and during that time, I learned a quite a few things about the big red horse that was traveling with us. At first, I thought she was a snob, but I soon found out she only acted that way because she was so nervous. She wasn't even sure what the new owner would call her, since she had never been called anything except her registered name, which is Impressive Exception. When Mr. B talked to her in the trailer, he called her Secret. That had a nice sound to me. Maybe he will make that her permanent everyday name. I think it's pretty cool! Different too!

It was getting pretty late by the time we finally arrived at the Diamond B Ranch. As we drove down the driveway to the barn, I noticed four horses looking out their stall windows. They all whinnied very loudly. I don't know if that was a welcoming party or if they were just happy to see Mr. B. Probably a bit of both. One thing was certain, I was glad to be at our final destination. It had been a long, exhausting day.

Our mister immediately unloaded us; he seemed to know that the trip was very hard on my young colt. Once we got settled in our fresh new stall, my little one curled up on the soft, sandy floor and went right to sleep.

Dee & Don Dee sleeping in pasture

Everything was wonderful—very clean and well organized. Mr. B promptly fed me some sweet grain, cool water, and lots of fresh-smelling hay. I hadn't anticipated that we would be lucky enough to end up in such a beautiful home. I was sure we would be happy in our new surroundings. I could see that Secret was also in a new stall, and she got the same treatment as we did.

All in all, I found the trip easy, but I was having a hard time trying to control my gas. I wanted to wait until my new owners left the barn, but it was getting harder by the minute. When most horses pass wind, it sounds like a human saying "afew, afew," but I have a big problem. When I toot, there's no hiding it. It just seems to explode all of a sudden, and it sounds like the Ryan Express rolling through. I kid you not. Sometimes it even scares me!

I felt like making an apology to the other horses before I did it, but I just couldn't wait any longer, so I just let it r-r-r-rip!

Dee & Don Dee in thier corral

Dee & Secret

Dee

Mr. B & Dee

The horse in the adjoining stall was called Texas, and he immediately started kicking the stall wall that separated us. Mr. B and his wife had been busy brushing Secret and discussing the business of the day. They were quite alarmed, especially when it lasted so long. They rushed over to me to make sure I hadn't busted something. I bet they were surprised to see that my tail was still connected.

My colt was used to this distraction, so he just slept right through all the excitement. It wasn't my intention to scare them all like that, but I couldn't hold it any longer. I don't think Texas ever forgave me.

The following day, Mr. B was there bright and early to feed all of us our grain and put us out to pasture. He had decided to call my young colt Don Dee. I really liked the name, and it certainly was different. Everything was just fantastic.

Today I feel so blessed that things turned out the way they did. It's a beautiful day. The sun is shining. There's a soft breeze and several acres of lush green pastures to explore, plus a large pond to bathe in. I know in my heart that this is to be my forever home.

Dee was right. Diamond B Ranch was her forever home. Sad to say, she passed away at the old age of twenty-four in July of 2014. She was a very sweet horse; we loved her dearly, and we miss her.

All Good Friends

Printed in the United States
By Bookmasters